Stinky

Compiled by
Barbara Ireson

Illustrated by Sue Heap

RED FOX

A Red Fox Book

Published by Random House Children's Books
20 Vauxhall Bridge Road, London SW1V 2SA

A division of Random House UK Ltd

London Melbourne Sydney Auckland Johannesburg
and agencies throughout the world

First published in 1992 by The Bodley Head Children's Books

Red Fox edition 1993

3 5 7 9 10 8 6 4

Text © in this collection Barbara Ireson 1992
Illustrations © Sue Heap 1992

The right of Barbara Ireson and Sue Heap to be identified
as the compiler and illustrator of this work have been
asserted by them in accordance with the Copyright,
Designs and Patents Act, 1988

Printed and bound in Great Britain by
Cox & Wyman Ltd, Reading, Berkshire

RANDOM HOUSE UK Limited Reg. No. 954009

ISBN 0 09 911241 8

Contents

1   The Chewing-Gum Rescue *teeth*.   1 ⁶⁄₁₀
    Margaret Mahy

2   Rattlesnake Soup   16
    Philip Ashton Rollins

3   How to Recognize a Witch *excerpt from The Witches*   19
    Roald Dahl

4   Toothie and Cat   31
    Gene Kemp

5   The Story of Giant Kippernose *smell*   40 ⁶
    John Cunliffe

6   Did I Ever Tell You . . . About the
    Dirtiest Children in the World *water clear*   51 ⁵
    Iris Grender

7   Guess   57
    Philippa Pearce

8   The Terrible Wild Grey Hairy Thing   70
    Jean Chapman

9   The Turbulent Term of Tyke Tiler   81
    Gene Kemp

The Chewing-Gum Rescue

Margaret Mahy

On the evening of pocket-money day Mr. Frisbee came stumping along to his own back door after shutting up his prize-winning angora goats, Gregorius and Gertrude, for the night. He had been very careful about this for the infamous Gargle Goat Thief Gang was roaming around the countryside, stealing goats of all kinds – very worrying for goat owners. Mr. Frisbee was looking forward to a quiet evening with his wife and children. But as he was wiping his weary feet in

1

their faithful gumboots, suddenly the gumboots stuck to the doormat and he fell head-over-heels into the hall.

'Help! Help!' shouted Mr. Frisbee as he lay there, his feet up in the air and the doormat still stuck to his boots. His five daughters, Florence, Flora, Fenella, Felicity and the baby Francesca came running to see what had happened to their loving father.

'Oh Dad!' cried Florence. 'You have trodden on a piece of Francesca's chewing-gum.'

'Yes,' said Flora. 'You know, Dad! It's on the telly.'

'It's on the doormat too,' grumbled Mr. Frisbee shaking his feet out of their faithful gumboots.

'It's advertised on television,' Flora explained. 'It's Dr. Gumption's simply Great Green Gum with the Daisy Fresh Mint Flavour.'

'It's full of fluoride and chlorophyll and it's the gum that's good for the gums,' said Felicity.

'And it's got champion chewability,' finished Fenella as she helped Felicity pull the doormat away from the gumboots. It took a lot of doing.

'Can't you have ice-cream instead?' asked Mr. Frisbee fretfully.

And Florence, Flora, Felicity, Fenella and even Francesca replied as one daughter, 'Mum won't let us.'

'Of course I won't,' said Mrs. Frisbee firmly, for she was a dentist during the day, and disapproved of sweets and cakes which, as everyone knows, are so bad for children's teeth. 'No ice-creams in this house, no chocolate or sherbert or coconut cream caramels or butterscotch! No fudge or toffee-apples, no brown sugar peanut brittle, and no buttery molasses taffy. Dr. Gumption's Gum is the only thing I'm prepared to tolerate. I want all my daughters to have teeth as strong as tigers' teeth and as beautiful as pearls.'

Well, that very night, after the girls had eaten all their greens, chewed their crusts twenty-five times each and had each finished off with a raw carrot, they sat down to watch television. But no sooner had the television set been switched on that Dr. Gumption himself appeared, smiling and scraping all over the screen.

'Hey kids!' he cried. 'It's good GOOD news. Dr. Gumption has a great new gum on the market and – WOW – it's twice as sticky and – mmmmmmmmmm – it's twice as stretchy and – YAY – it's twice as green and it's got double that super duper minty flavour, so listen kids, to what everyone is saying. . . .'

And then a chorus of beautiful girls in green clustered around Dr. Gumption and they sang . . .

'Do friends avoid you? Take that hint!
Chew Dr. Gumption's Minty-mint.'

'Shall we?' Florence signalled to her sisters by wiggling her crooked eyebrows.

'Next pocket-money day!' Flora signalled back with hers.

Next pocket-money day Mr. Frisbee came home after locking up his prize angora goats with tremendous care and he found that the back door wouldn't even open; he had to go round to the front door like a polite visitor. As he came in the smell of minty-mint rolled towards him like a great green ocean.

'What's happened to the back door?' he demanded crossly.

'It's got a piece of Felicity's gum stuck in it,' said Flora, telling tales as she often did.

'Fenella made me put it there,' grumbled Felicity. 'She said . . . "Just for fun put your gum here!" and when I did, she shut the door on it and now we can't get the door open, and my gum has gone for good.'

'Honestly, my dear,' Mr. Frisbee said to his wife, 'a simple orange each would save a lot of trouble in the long run.'

'Never!' declared Mrs. Frisbee (Dentist). 'I spend all day patching up teeth ruined by coconut candy and frosted cakes. Never shall my daughters feast on brandy balls or barley sugar,

5

Turkish delight, marshmallows or chocolate peanuts. They shall have teeth as strong as tigers' teeth and as beautiful as pearls.'

But later, when the lid of the piano refused to open because Francesca's gum was jammed under it, Mrs. Frisbee looked very thoughtful and still later, when the tablecloth stuck to the table just as if it had been nailed at all four corners, she looked quite cross.

That very night on television the beaming face of Dr. Gumption appeared once more.

'Hey kids, hey!' he shouted. 'Boy oh boy! What news! Dr. Gumption's Gum has been improved yet again. Triple Chewability! Quadruple stretch power. Ten times the stickability! Oh that gloptious Gumption Gum. It's the NOW gum! It's the POW gum! And don't forget, kids, it's got that triple ripple super duper minty-mint flavour.' And the girls in green appeared and sang . . .

'Make your father go all numb!
Chew Dr. Gumption's Gloptious Gum!'

'Shall we?' signalled Florence with her crooked eyebrows.

'Yes, yes, yes!' signalled Flora, Felicity, Fenella, and Francesca.

A week later on pocket-money day Mr. Frisbee came home having shut his precious Gregorious and Gertrude away for the night.

'The Gargle Gang will never get them,' he muttered fiercely to himself. 'But locking up is hard work. I'm longing for a cup of tea.' He stumped up the path in his faithful gumboots but he could not open the back door or the front door either. Most of the windows were sealed shut, too, but at last he found that he could open the bathroom window with a stick, and by standing on an up-ended apple box he was able to somersault into his house.

Inside, the smell of Super Duper Minty-mint was so strong he staggered back clutching his throat. Dr. Gumption's chewing-gum stretched everywhere in an evil green web. It was as if a whole houseful of wicked spiders had been at work for a week. It seized your shoes and stuck them to the floor, it caught your coat and held on to your hair. It was like a super duper minty-mint mad monster from Mars stretching from room to room to room to room.

'Arrrrrh!' cried Mr. Frisbee, as his five daughters and Mrs. Frisbee came to meet him, climbing nimbly through the sticky maze. 'Couldn't you let them have a liquorice all-sort each instead?' he gasped.

'No, no!' replied Mrs Frisbee. 'I'm a dentist as well as a mother. If you saw the horrors that I see every day – molars molested and melted away by refined sugars – you would understand.

Never shall my little ones have peppermint creams or coconut ice, boiled lollies, dolly mixtures, raspberry drops, wine gums, humbugs, jujubes or all-day suckers. My daughters must have teeth as strong as tiger's teeth and as beautiful as pearls.'

'I suppose they must,' said Mr. Frisbee wearily.

At dinner that night the soup tasted of Dr. Gumption's Super Duper Minty-mint Gum. The roast beef, roast potatoes, roast onions, roast parsnips, roast pumpkin and buttered beans all tasted of Dr. Gumption's Super Duper Minty-mint Gum and so did the wholesome apple brown-betty and the raw carrots to finish off with. No one enjoyed anything very much.

Yet that very night on television Dr. Gumption appeared again. 'Hey kids!' he shouted. 'Hey – all you gum chewers out there! Have you tried Dr. Gumption's NEW splendiferous magniferous gum? Such expansion. Such extension! It stretches up and out and every whichever way. It's the fun gum that keeps the household happy and healthy. It sticks so well that it's being used by boat builders as a saltwater glue. And it's got that unutterable, that entirely inexpressible super duper triple ripple more-minty-than-mint flavour. WOW!'

Then the girls in green appeared and sang . . .

'Want to make your teacher squint?
Chew Dr. Gumption's Minty-mint.'

'Next time!' Florence signalled Flora, Felicity,
Fenella and Francesca, wiggling her eyebrows in
time to the music.

A week later on pocket-money day Mr. Frisbee staggered up to bed coughing and choking
and fighting off green tentacles of gum.

'Man can triumph over any odds,' he muttered. 'He can get used to anything if he has to.'
He was a bit lonely because Mrs. Frisbee was
out at a Dental Health Conference.

What Mr. Frisbee did not know was that Florence, Flora, Felicity, Fenella and even Francesca
all had packets of Dr. Gumption's New More-
minty-than-mint Gum tucked under their pillows. They hadn't started chewing it yet because
they had some of the old Triple Minty-mint Gum
from last week's pocket-money day to use up
first.

As he lay awake, missing Mrs. Frisbee
B.D.S., Mr. Frisbee heard strange shufflings
and muffled bleats coming from the goat pens.
They were not very loud and, had Mrs. Frisbee
been at home, he would have been sound asleep
and would have missed hearing them altogether.
As it was he leaped to his feet and peeped out
of the window. What a sight met his eyes!

There were the five dreadful Gargle brothers,

leaders of the Gargle Goat Thief Gang, not to mention five of their minions. They were in the actual act of stealing Gregorius and Gertrude, Mr. Frisbee's prize-winning angoras. There was not a moment to be lost.

Wrapping his hands in Mrs. Frisbee's second-best petticoat and seizing a strand of Doctor Gumption's Triple Super Duper Minty-mint Gum that happened to be dangling from the guttering, Mr.Frisbee swung down like Tarzan, a curiously splendid figure in his simulated leopardskin pyjamas, screaming reprimands and reproaches at the villainous goat thieves.

Florence and Flora woke up at once and looked out of the window. What they saw horrified them and they hastened to wake up Felicity, Fenella and even Francesca by way of reinforcements. Armed only with Dr. Gumption's New More-minty-than-mint Gum, they climbed out of the bathroom window and whisked over to the goat pens.

For there was no doubt that Mr. Frisbee was getting the worst of it.

In his first spectacular swing he had struck Harvey Gargle to the ground and then as he swept majestically back he had struck Ellis Gargle, knocking out his false teeth and seriously bewildering him. But then he himself hit the side of the house very hard and let go of the chewing-gum, falling dazed to the ground, an

10

easy prey to the infuriated goat thieves.

Mad Rory Gargle with two minions advanced upon him in a threatening way; Bernard Gargle (with two other minions) picked up his fallen brothers, not forgetting Ellis's false teeth, while Rackham Gargle with the single remaining minion rapidly led Gregorious Goat and his nanny wife, Gertrude, towards a waiting van.

Victory was within the grasp of the nefarious goat thieves. All seemed lost . . .

When, suddenly, with a lion-like roar Florence sprang out at them from the right, biting firmly into a piece of Dr. Gumption's New More-minty-than-mint gum as she did so. Flora bounded in from the left, whooping and hooting like a whole treeful of owls. There was a hearty hullabaloo from Fenella who, chewing her piece of Dr. Gumption's Mintier-than-mint Gum, came up behind Florence, a blood-curdling growl from Felicity leaping out of the chrysanthemums, and squeaks and squeals from Francesca who rose up out of the watering-can.

The goat thieves were entirely taken aback. This unexpected racket and rumpus-bumpus upset them badly.

'Squad . . . breathe OUT!' shouted Florence and the daughters of the house breathed out as one combined daughter. A terrible wave of unutterable, indescribable, inexpressible, super duper triple ripple more-minty-than-mint aroma

swept over the goat thieves.

'Enemy Mint Gas Attack!' shouted Mad Rory Gargle before he dropped like a stone. Lewis and Rackham Gargle and the assorted minions keeled over like slender reeds in a hurricane and even the goats fell to their knees gasping.

Mr. Frisbee, however, had been exposed to Dr. Gumption's punishing mint flavour for at least three weeks and although somewhat unsteady, he was not totally overcome. He had built up an immunity.

'Tie them up!' he ordered. 'Quickly.'

His devoted daughters did not hesitate. Within a moment the Gargle Gang were wound around with Dr. Gumption's powerful product. The music died down and the goats began to revive. At this very moment Mrs. Frisbee drove the family car into the yard. She was astonished to find it filled with disabled goat thieves, groggy goats, her husband bruised but resplendent in his simulated leopardskin pyjamas, not to mention her five daughters still up well beyond their bedtime.

'You see how wise I was,' she said. 'You couldn't have saved Gregorius and Gertrude with a piece of Turkish delight.'

'I'll never say anything against Dr. Gumption's Mintier-than-mint Gum again,' Mr. Frisbee vowed fervently.

Florence looked at her sisters. 'Shall I tell

him?' she signalled with her crooked eyebrows.

'O.K.,' they all signalled back.

'Actually Dad,' said Florence, 'we're getting rather sick of it.'

'Well, that's all right, my dear,' said Mrs. Frisbee quickly, 'because I heard of a delicious new sweet at the Conference today. Honey Bliss it's called and it's made with pure golden honey collected from lime blossoms by particularly happy and busy bees. Of course you'll still have to brush your teeth after it, but you have to do that anyway.'

Florence, Flora, Felicity, Fenella and Francesca looked delighted to hear this. They had enjoyed Dr. Gumption's Gum but it was very hard work keeping it under control and they needed a rest.

The police came and took the goat thieves away. 'We've been waiting a long time to get our hands on this lot,' the Chief Constable said. 'There's a big reward, you know. You'll be able to extend your herd of angora goats.'

Mr. Frisbee, though bruised and battered, beamed with joy.

Shortly after this Dr. Gumption's Gum was withdrawn from the market and only used again in army exercises. Florence, Flora, Felicity, Fenella and Francesca settled down with Honey Bliss which smelt deliciously of lime blossom and tasted wonderful. However, it must be noted that when Gertrude the goat had two beautiful kids a short time later they did have, very faintly, a mintier-than-mint perfume, no doubt due to their mother's exposure to Dr. Gumption's Gum during the great mintier-than-mint goat rescue and the heroic victory of the Frisbee's sisters, all of whom grew up to have teeth as strong as tigers' teeth and as beautiful as pearls.

Rattlesnake Soup

Philip Ashton Rollins

For a meal you will never forget, try some thick, chunky rattlesnake soup, brimming over with big juicy pieces of freshly killed rattlesnake. It's a lot of trouble to make, but it's worth it.

You will need a gallon-size bucket and a quart-size can, the kind tomatoes come in. The bucket should be slightly rusty on the inside, to add the right amount of iron to the soup. Just be sure the rust doesn't go all the way through, or the

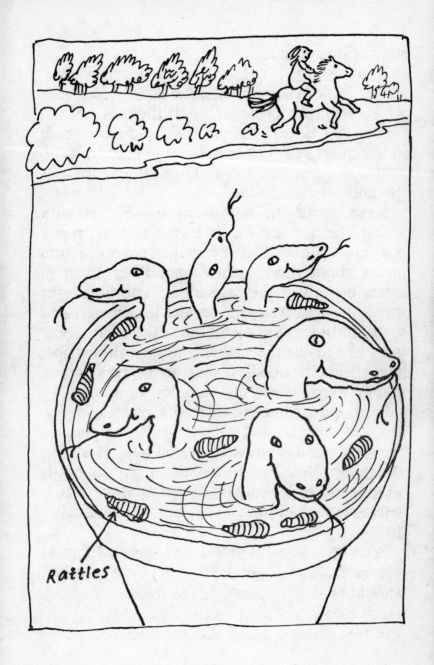

Rattles

soup will leak out.

You also will need about a dozen young, tender rattlesnakes and about a dozen older ones with a stronger flavour. Cut off the heads of the snakes just behind the ear slits, and store them in the quart can. Cover them with cold water to keep them nice and fresh. Then remove the rattles and set them aside.

Next, cover the bottom of the bucket with young, tender sagebrush leaves and a prickly pear cut up fine. Cut the snakes crosswise into pieces about three inches long. Place them in layers on top of the sagebrush. The first layer should be crosswise, the second lengthwise, and so on, until you use up all the snake meat. Some folks like to cut the snakes into long thin strips, like spaghetti noodles, but that gives you a stringy soup instead of a chunky soup.

Now, add some blackstrap molasses, a few drops of vinegar, and as much salt, red pepper, black pepper and mustard as you like. Mix it up with a big stick. For a decoration, put the heads on top, sort of looking up at you, and the rattles in a circle around them. That should look mighty pretty.

Then get on your horse and out of there as fast as you can, and leave the whole stinkin' mess behind.

How to Recognize a Witch

Roald Dahl

The next evening after my grandmother had given me my bath, she took me once again into the living room for another story.

'Tonight,' the old woman said, 'I am going to tell you how to recognize a witch when you see one.'

'Can you always be sure?' I asked.

'No,' she said, 'you can't. And that's the trouble. But you can make a pretty good guess.'

She was dropping cigar ash all over her lap,

and I hoped she wasn't going to catch on fire before she'd told me how to recognize a witch.

'In the first place,' she said, 'a REAL WITCH is certain always to be wearing gloves when you meet her.'

'Surely not *always*,' I said. 'What about in the summer when it's hot?'

'Even in the summer,' my grandmother said. 'She has to. Do you want to know why?'

'Why?' I said.

'Because she doesn't have fingernails. Instead of fingernails, she has thin curvy claws, like a cat, and she wears the gloves to hide them. Mind you, lots of very respectable women wear gloves, especially in winter, so this doesn't help you very much.'

'Mamma used to wear gloves,' I said.

'Not in the house,' my grandmother said. 'Witches wear gloves even in the house. They only take them off when they go to bed.'

'How do you know all this, Grandmamma?'

'Don't interrupt,' she said. 'Just take it all in. The second thing to remember is that a REAL WITCH is always bald.'

'*Bald*?' I said.

'Bald as a boiled egg,' my grandmother said.

I was shocked. There was something indecent about a bald woman. 'Why are they bald, Grandmamma?'

'Don't ask me why,' she snapped. 'But you

can take it from me that not a single hair grows on a witch's head.'

'How horrid!'

'Disgusting,' my grandmother said.

'If she's bald, she'll be easy to spot,' I said.

'Not at all,' my grandmother said. 'A REAL WITCH always wears a wig to hide her baldness. She wears a first-class wig. And it is almost impossible to tell a really first-class wig from ordinary hair unless you give it a pull to see if it comes off.'

'Then that's what I'll have to do,' I said.

'Don't be foolish,' my grandmother said. 'You can't go around pulling at the hair of every lady you meet, even if she is wearing gloves. Just try it and see what happens.'

'So that doesn't help much either,' I said.

'None of these things is any good on its own,' my grandmother said. 'It's only when you put them all together that they begin to make a little sense. Mind you,' my grandmother went on, 'these wigs do cause a rather serious problem for witches.'

'What problem, Grandmamma?'

'They make the scalp itch most terribly,' she said. 'You see, when an actress wears a wig, or if you or I were to wear a wig, we would be putting it on over our own hair, but a witch has to put it straight onto her naked scalp. And the underneath of a wig is always very rough and

scratchy. It sets up a frightful itch on the bald skin. It causes nasty sores on the head. Wigrash, the witches call it. And it doesn't half itch.'

'What other things must I look for to recognize a witch?' I asked.

'Look for the nose-holes,' my grandmother said. 'Witches have slightly larger nose-holes than ordinary people. The rim of each nose-hole is pink and curvy, like the rim of a certain kind of seashell.'

'Why do they have such big nose-holes?' I asked.

'For smelling with,' my grandmother said. 'A REAL WITCH has the most amazing powers of smell. She can actually smell out a child who is standing on the other side of the street on a pitch-black night.'

'She couldn't smell me,' I said. 'I've just had a bath.'

'Oh yes she could,' my grandmother said. 'The cleaner you happen to be, the more smelly you are to a witch.'

'That can't be true,' I said.

'An absolutely clean child gives off the most ghastly stench to a witch,' my grandmother said. 'The dirtier you are, the less you smell.'

'But that doesn't make sense, Grandmamma.'

'Oh yes it does,' my grandmother said. 'It isn't the *dirt* that the witch is smelling. It is *you*. The smell that drives a witch mad actually comes right out of your own skin. It comes oozing out of your skin in waves, and these waves – stink-waves, the witches call them – go floating through the air and hit the witch right smack in her nostrils. They send her reeling.'

'Now wait a minute, Grandmamma . . .'

'Don't interrupt,' she said. 'The point is this. When you haven't washed for a week and your skin is all covered over with dirt, then quite obviously the stink-waves cannot come oozing out nearly so strongly.'

'I shall never have a bath again,' I said.

'Just don't have one too often,' my grandmother said. 'Once a month is quite enough for a sensible child.'

It was at moments like these that I loved my grandmother more than ever.

'Grandmamma,' I said, 'if it's a dark night, how can a witch smell the difference between a child and a grownup?'

'Because grownups don't give out stink-waves,' she said. 'Only children do that.'

'But I don't *really* give out stink-waves, do I?' I said. 'I'm not giving them out at this very moment, am I?'

'Not to me you aren't,' my grandmother said. 'To me you are smelling like raspberries and cream. But to a witch you would be smelling absolutely disgusting.'

'What would I be smelling of?' I asked.

'Dogs' droppings,' my grandmother said.

I reeled. I was stunned. '*Dogs' droppings!*' I cried. 'I am *not* smelling of dogs' droppings! I don't believe it! I *won't* believe it!'

'What's more,' my grandmother said, speaking with a touch of relish, 'to a witch you'd be smelling of *fresh* dog's droppings.'

'That simply is not true!' I cried. 'I know I am not smelling of dogs' droppings, stale or fresh!'

'There's no point in arguing about it,' my grandmother said. 'It's a fact of life.'

I was outraged. I simply couldn't bring myself to believe what my grandmother was telling me.

'So if you see a woman holding her nose as she passes you in the street,' she went on, 'that woman could easily be a witch.'

I decided to change the subject. 'Tell me what else to look for in a witch,' I said.

'The eyes,' my grandmother said. 'Look carefully at the eyes, because the eyes of a REAL WITCH are different from yours and mine. Look in the middle of each eye where there is normally a little black dot. If she is a witch, the black dot will keep changing colour, and you will see fire and you will see ice dancing right in the very centre of the coloured dot. It will send shivers running all over your skin.'

My grandmother leaned back in her chair and sucked away contentedly at her foul black cigar.

I squatted on the floor, staring up at her, fascinated. She was not smiling. She looked deadly serious.

'Are there other things?' I asked her.

'Of course there are other things,' my grandmother said. 'You don't seem to understand that witches are not actually human beings at all. They *look* like humans. They talk like humans. And they are able to act like humans. But in actual fact, they are totally different animals. They are demons in human shape. That is why they have claws and bald heads and queer noses and peculiar eyes, all of which they have to conceal as best they can from the rest of the world.'

'What else is different about them, Grandmamma?'

'The feet,' she said. 'Witches never have toes.'

'No toes!' I cried. 'Then what do they have?'

'They just have feet,' my grandmother said. 'The feet have square ends with no toes on them at all.'

'Does that make it difficult to walk?' I asked.

'Not at all,' my grandmother said. 'But it does give them a problem with their shoes. All ladies like to wear small, rather pointed shoes, but a witch, whose feet are very wide and square at the ends, has the most awful job squeezing her feet into those neat little pointed shoes.'

'Why doesn't she wear wide comfy shoes with square ends?' I asked.

'She dare not,' my grandmother said. 'Just as she hides her baldness with a wig, she must also hide her ugly witch's feet by squeezing them into pretty shoes.'

'Isn't that terribly uncomfortable?' I said.

'Extremely uncomfortable,' my grandmother said. 'But she has to put up with it.'

'If she's wearing ordinary shoes, it won't help me to recognize her, will it, Grandmamma?'

'I'm afraid it won't,' my grandmother said. 'You might possibly see her limping very slightly, but only if you were watching closely.'

'Are those the only differences then, Grandmamma?'

'There's one more,' my grandmother said. 'Just one more.'

'What is it, Grandmamma?'

'Their spit is blue.'

'Blue!' I cried. 'Not blue! Their spit can't be *blue*!'

'Blue as a bilberry,' she said.

'You don't mean it, Grandmamma! Nobody can have blue spit!'

'Witches can,' she said.

'Is it like ink?' I asked.

'Exactly,' she said. 'They even use it to write with. They use those old-fashioned pens that have nibs and they simply lick the nib.'

'Can you *notice* the blue spit, Grandmamma? If a witch was talking to me, would I be able to notice it?'

'Only if you looked carefully,' my grandmother said. 'If you looked very carefully you would probably see a slight bluish tinge on her teeth. But it doesn't show much.'

'It would if she spat,' I said.

'Witches never spit,' my grandmother said. 'They daren't.'

I couldn't believe my grandmother would be lying to me. She went to church every morning of the week and she said grace before every meal, and somebody who did that would never tell lies. I was beginning to believe every word she spoke.

'So there you are,' my grandmother said. 'That's about all I can tell you. None of it is very helpful. You can still never be absolutely sure whether a woman is a witch or not just by looking at her. But if she is wearing the gloves, if she has the large nose holes, the queer eyes, and hair that looks as though it might be a wig, and if she has a bluish tinge on her teeth – if she has all of these things, then you run like mad.'

'Grandmamma,' I said, 'when you were a little girl, did *you* ever meet a witch?'

'Once,' my grandmother said. 'Only once.'

'What happened?'

'I'm not going to tell you,' she said. 'It would frighten you out of your skin and give you bad

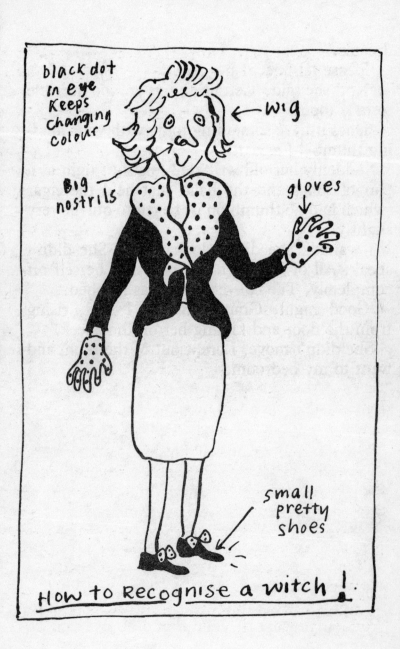

dreams.'

'Please tell me,' I begged.

'No,' she said. 'Certain things are too horrible to talk about.'

'Does it have something to do with your missing thumb?' I asked.

Suddenly her old wrinkled lips shut tight as a pair of tongs and the hand that held the cigar (which had no thumb on it) began to quiver very slightly.

I waited. She didn't look at me. She didn't speak. All of a sudden she had shut herself off completely. The conversation was finished.

'Good night, Grandmamma,' I said, rising from the floor and kissing her on the cheek.

She didn't move. I crept out of the room and went to my bedroom.

Toothie And Cat

Gene Kemp

High on the hills above the city was a cave, well hidden away among the trees and the rocks and the bracken. And in that cave lived an old tramp with a gingery, greyish beard hanging to his waist, a greasy hat on his head, string tied just below the knees of his trousers, and one tooth that stuck out over his beard. Because of this he was known as Toothie, and he couldn't remember any other name. He couldn't remember very much at all, for his brain was as foggy

31

as a November night. He was never bright even in his prime and he hadn't improved with the years. Nobody had ever cared for him much ever since his mother dumped him, wrapped in an old blanket, outside a police station, and then made off as fast as she could. Toothie tried to keep away from police stations ever after.

Below the hills in the city lived Cat. Cat the Black and the Bad, a streak of a cat with claws as sharp as daggers and a heart as black as his tatty fur. No one loved Cat. Once he was dropped in a river and left to drown. But you don't drown animals like Cat that easily. He got out, and survived, by hatred, mostly. He hated people and children and bright lights and kindness. He loved fighting and stealing, roof-tops and alleys, and, most of all, dustbins. He relied on them when the birds grew careful, or too many kitchen doors were shut. In the daytime he thieved and slept on walls in patches of sunlight. At night he rampaged across roof-tops, wailing and caterwauling. So he lived for some years, till one morning he dropped from a roof-top a bit carelessly, and a car speeding through the dawn grazed his leg. Snarling and swearing, he limped to the side of the road, where Toothie, who had also been raiding dustbins, found him. He was pleased, for he'd found a very meaty chicken carcase.

He walked all round Cat, who spat at him.

Then he popped a bit of chicken into the complaining mouth, and Cat stopped spitting, and ate instead. Toothie popped him in his old bag, and went back to the cave, where he made some chicken soup and tied a big leaf round the injured leg. After a time Cat stopped spitting at him, for he'd grown to like Toothie's smell. His leg healed.

Cat did not return to the city. It was summer. He hunted and Toothie cooked: stews and soups in his iron pot, other tasty dishes baked in mud packed at the base of the fire. Long warm days passed by in the green wood and the dark cave. Sometimes Toothie would sing and Cat purr, both rusty noises. That autumn was beautiful, warm and golden, with more nuts than had been seen for years. Toothie and Cat were well fed and content.

Until the night the October wind arrived, blowing cold, stripping the leaves off the trees, and it brought with it the sound of cats singing in the city below. Cat stirred in his sleep and woke up. He left Toothie's warmth to sit in the mouth of the cave, listening. Yes, there, again, came the yowling of cats. Cat shivered. He looked once at the old man, asleep, and slipped out into the night.

A fortnight later he came back, hungry, limping, wet and exhausted, longing for Toothie's warm fire, Toothie's food, Toothie's smelly com-

pany. But the cave was empty. The iron pot hung forlornly by the burnt-out fire. Toothie had gone.

Cat sat and washed himself, which is what cats do when they don't know what to do next. Then he searched through the woods, crying his strange, wild call. There was no Toothie. Cat slew an unwary bird who would have done better to have migrated and, still hungry, set off for the city.

Through the streets he ran, sniffing, investigating, fighting, always searching for Toothie's fascinating smell, and one day, a week or so later, he arrived at the City Hospital and knew that his friend was inside.

Now Cat was much cleverer than Toothie, and he knew from the smell of the hospital that that was where people were ill, and his cat brain put illness and chicken together. He'd got to find some chicken.

He tried as many houses as he had paws before he finally crept into a gleaming, shiny bright kitchen, and there on the immaculate tiled surface lay a scrumptious chicken leg on a plate of crisp salad. The salad Cat ignored, he was not a lettuce-eater, but he seized the chicken and was just about to leap through the partially open window when the owner appeared, screamed like a whistling kettle and spent the rest of the day feeling very ill indeed, and telling anyone who could be made to listen how a fiendish monster had appeared like a black demon in her sacred kitchen. Cat kept increasing in size till he reached the dimensions of a mini-tiger.

A while later, the mini-tiger sat outside the hospital door and waited, chicken portion gripped firmly in teeth. Going in at the front door didn't seem like a good idea – it looked too busy and important. Cat had never liked front doors, anyway. Back or side doors were for the likes of him. So he slunk round the corner till he came to a dark staircase that went up and up and on and on. Right at the top were dozens of dustbins. Cat purred through the chicken. He liked those dustbins, homely and friendly, they were.

Beyond them was a door with two little round glass panels. It opened in the middle and swung as someone walked through. And Cat slid in, keeping a very low profile. He ran, chicken in mouth and stomach almost on the floor, through rows of beds, and then into another ward with yet more beds. In the third a little boy lay in bed, bored. He sat up and cried:

'There's a cat. It's got something in its mouth. Good ole puss cat. Come here.'

He wanted Cat a lot, but Cat ran on. But now that he was spotted, pandemonium broke loose.

'Catch that cat!'

'Stop him!'

'Get that filthy animal out of here!'

As fast as he could, Cat ran on. Patients shouted as nurses ran to grab him.

But nothing could stop Cat now. Like a rocket swooshing into space, Cat shot down the ward to find Toothie. He dodged trolleys, ran under beds, ran over beds, squeezed between legs, narrowly missed cleaners, tripped up nurses carrying vases of flowers or trays, scattering people right and left to reach the bed with the screens round it where Toothie lay.

He'd collapsed with pneumonia a week after Cat had left him and somehow, shivering, coughing, full of pains, he'd crawled to the road, where a bus driver had driven him straight to the hospital despite complaints from some of the passengers. And since then, Toothie had lain in terror of the bright lights, the uniforms, the smells and the sounds, all too much for his mazed mind. He wanted to die.

Sister's voice rang out loud and clear.

'Stop that beast! It's got germs!'

Hands grabbed at Cat, missing narrowly. He shot through the screens and the doctor and nurses beside Toothie and up on to the bed. There on the whiter than white, brighter than bright, snowy, frosty, bleached, purified, disinfected, sterilized, decontaminated pillow Cat laid the dusty, greasy, tooth-marked chicken leg, just beside Toothie's head.

Shouts were all about him.

But Toothie's eyes opened and he saw Cat. A triumphant burst of purring sounded through the ward. Come what might, Cat had arrived. He'd found Toothie.

The Story of
Giant Kippernose

John Cunliffe

Once there was a giant called Kippernose. He lived on a lonely farm in the mountains. He was not fierce. Indeed he was as kind and as gentle as a giant could be. He liked children, and was fond of animals. He was good at telling stories. His favourite foods were ice-cream, cakes, lollipops and sausages. He would help anyone, large or small. And yet he had no friends. When he went to the town to do his shopping, everyone ran away from him. Busy

40

streets emptied in a trice. Everyone ran home, bolted their doors and closed all their windows, even on hot summer days.

Kippernose shouted.

'Don't run away! I'll not hurt you! Please don't run away, I like little people. I've only come to do my shopping. Please come out. I'll tell you a good story about a dragon and a mermaid.'

But it was no use. The town stayed silent and empty; the doors and windows stayed firmly closed. Poor Kippernose wanted so much to have someone to talk to. He felt so lonely that he often sat down in the town square and cried his heart out. You would think someone would take pity on him, but no one ever did. He simply couldn't understand it. He even tried going to another town, far across the mountains, but just the same thing happened.

'Has all the world gone mad?' said Kippernose to himself, and took his solitary way home.

The truth was that the people were not afraid of Kippernose, and they had not gone mad, either. The truth *was* . . . that Kippernose had not had a single bath in a hundred years, or more! The poor fellow carried such a stink wherever he went that everyone with a nose on his face ran for cover at the first whiff. Oh, how that giant reeked! Pooh, you could smell him a mile away, and worst of all on hot days. People buried

their noses in flowers and lavender-bags, but still the stench crept in. The wives cried shame and shame upon him, and swore that his stink turned their milk sour, and their butter rancid. What made matters worse, he never washed his hair or his whiskers, either. Smelly whiskers bristled all over his chin, and little creatures crept amongst them. His greasy hair fell down his back. He never used a comb. He never brushed his teeth. *And*, quite often, he went to bed with his boots on.

When he was a boy, Kippernose was always clean and smart, his mother saw to that. Long long ago, his good mother had gone off to live in far Cathay, and he had forgotten all she had told him about keeping clean and tidy, and changing his socks once a week. It was a lucky thing when his socks wore out, because that was the only time he would change them. He had no notion of the sight and smell he was. He never looked in a mirror. His smell had grown up with him, and he didn't notice it at all. His mind was deep among tales of dragons and wizards, for people in stories were his only friends. If only someone could have told him about his smell, in a nice way, all would have been well. The people grumbled enough amongst themselves. Mrs Dobson, of Ivy Cottage, was one of them. Friday was market day, and ironing day too, and every Friday night she would bang her iron angrily, and say to quiet Mr Dobson by the fireside,

'That giant's a scandal. It's every market day we have the sickening stench of him, and the whole pantry turned sour and rotten, too. Can't you men do something about it? You sit there and warm your toes, and nod off to sleep, while the world's going to ruin . . .'

'But, Bessie, my dear,' mild Mr Dobson answered, 'what can we do? You cannot expect anyone to go up to an enormous giant and say, "I say, old chap, you smell most dreadfully" – now can you? Besides, no one could get near enough to him: the smell would drive them away.'

'You could send him a letter,' said Mrs Dobson.

'But he cannot read. He never went to school. Even as a boy, Kippernose was too big to get through the school door, my old grandfather used to say.'

'Well the government should do something about it,' said Mrs Dobson, banging on. 'If that Queen of ours came out of her palace and took a sniff of our Kippernose, *she'd* do something quickly enough, I'll bet.'

But it was not the Queen, or the government, or Mr Dobson, who solved the problem in the end. It was a creature so small that no one could see it.

One Friday in the middle of winter, a cold

day of ice and fog, Kippernose went to town to do his shopping as usual. He felt so unhappy that he didn't even bother to call out and ask the people to stay to talk to him. He just walked gloomily into the market-place.

'It's no good,' he said to himself, 'they'll never be friends with me. They don't seem to think a giant has feelings like anyone else, I might just as well be . . .'

'Hoi! Look where you're going!' an angry voice shouted up from the foggy street. 'Oh, I say, oh, help!' Then there was a great crash, and there were apples rolling everywhere. Then a babble of voices gathered round Kippernose.

'The clumsy great oaf – look, he's knocked Jim Surtees's apple-cart over. Did you ever see such a mess? Tramping about, not looking where he's going, with his head in the sky.'

Amongst all this angry noise stood Kipper-nose, with an enormous smile spreading across his big face. The smile grew to a grin.

'*They're not running away*. They're *not running away*,' said Kippernose, in a joyous whisper. Then he bent down, right down, and got down on his knees to bring his face near to the people.

'Why aren't you running away from me?' he said, softly, so as not to frighten them. 'Why aren't you running away as you always do? Please tell me, I beg of you.'

Jim Surtees was so angry that he had no fear

of Kippernose, and he climbed upon his over-turned apple-cart, and shouted up at him,

'Why, you great fool, it's because we cannot *smell* you.'

'Smell?' said Kippernose, puzzled.

'Yes; smell, stink, pong, stench; call it what you like,' said Jim.

'But I don't smell,' said Kippernose.

'Oh, yes you do!' all the people shouted together.

'You stink,' shouted Jim. 'You stink to the very heavens. That's why everyone runs away from you. It's too much for us – we just *have* to run away.'

'Why can't you smell me today?' said Kippernose.

'Because we've all caught a cold in the head for the first time in our lives, and our noses are stuffed up and runny, and we cannot smell anything, that's why,' said Jim. 'Some merchant came from England, selling ribbons, and gave us his germs as well. So we cannot smell you today, but next week we'll be better, and then see how we'll run.'

'But what can I do?' said Kippernose, looking so sad that even Jim felt sorry for him. 'I'm so lonely, with no one to talk to.'

'Well, you could take a bath,' said Jim.

'And you could wash your whiskers,' said Mrs Dobson. '. . . And your hair,' she added.

'*And* you could wash your clothes,' said Mr Dobson.

'*And* change your socks,' said Mrs Fox, eyeing his feet.

Distant memories stirred in Kippernose's head. 'Yes. Oh . . . yes. Mother did say something about all that, once, long ago; but I didn't take much notice. Do I really smell as bad as all that? Do I really?'

'Oh yes, you certainly do,' said Mrs Dobson. 'You smell a good deal worse than you can imagine. You turned my cheese green last week, *and* made Mrs Hill's baby cry for two hours without stopping when she left a window open by mistake. Oh, yes, you smell badly, Kippernose, as badly as anything could smell in this world.'

'If I do all you say, if I get all neat and clean, will you stop running away and be friends?' said Kippernose.

'Of course we will,' said Jim Surtees. 'We have nothing against giants. They can be useful if only they'll look where they're putting their feet, and they do say the giants were the best story-tellers in the old days.'

'Just you wait and see,' shouted Kippernose. As soon as he had filled his shopping basket, he walked purposefully off towards the hills. In his basket were one hundred and twenty bars of soap, and fifty bottles of bubble-bath!

That night Kippernose was busy as never before. Fires roared, and hot water gurgled in all the pipes of his house. There was such a steaming, and a splashing, and a gasping, and a bubbling, and a lathering, and a singing, and a laughing, as had not been heard in Kippernose's house for a hundred years. A smell of soap and bubble-bath drifted out upon the air, and even as far away as the town, people caught a whiff of it.

'What's that lovely smell?' said Mrs Dobson to her husband. 'There's a beautifully clean and scented smell that makes me think of a summer garden, even though it is the middle of winter.'

Then there was a bonfire of dirty old clothes in a field near Kippernose's farm, and a snip-snipping of hair and whiskers. Then there was a great rummaging in drawers and cupboards, and a shaking and airing of fresh clothes. The whole of that week, Kippernose was busy, so busy that he almost forgot to sleep and eat.

When Friday came round again, the people of the town saw an astonishing sight. Dressed in a neat Sunday suit, clean and clipped, shining in the wintry sun, and smelling of soap and sweet lavender, Kippernose strode towards them. He was a new Kippernose. The people crowded round him, and Jim Surtees shouted,

'Is it really you, Kippernose?'

'It certainly is,' said Kippernose, beaming

joyously.

'Then you're welcome amongst us,' said Jim. 'You smell as sweetly as a flower, indeed you do, and I never thought you'd do it. Three cheers for good old Kippernose! Hip. Hip.'

And the crowd cheered,

'Hooray! Hooray! Hooray!'

Kippernose was never short of friends after that. He was so good and kind that all the people loved him, and he became the happiest giant in all the world.

Ever afterwards, if any children would not go in the bath, or wash, or brush their teeth, or have their hair cut . . . then their mothers would tell them the story of Giant Kippernose.

Did I Ever Tell You About the Dirtiest Children in the World?

Iris Grender

Now there is one thing that all mothers really like, and that is keeping their children clean. After a bath they search all the creases and crevices. Ears are the favourite things to search, which is strange because you can't even see inside them yourself, and only your own mother ever looks down inside them.

On the first morning we went to stay with Mr

and Mrs Farmer Jones, Mrs Farmer Jones took us outside and showed us where to wash ourselves. Francis and I had never seen anything like it before. There was a pump standing in a thing like a concrete sink on the ground. Mrs Farmer Jones pumped the handle up and down. At first nothing happened. All of a sudden water gushed out of the spout into the sink.

'That looks good,' said Francis. 'Can we have a bath in it?'

'If you want,' replied Mrs Farmer Jones, and with that she disappeared indoors. Francis pumped the handle up and down and each time a great jet of water shot into the sink.

I put my hands under the water. 'Ouch,' I squealed. It was the iciest water that ever was. Francis put his hand under the pump. All he said was, 'Crikey.'

I dared Francis to have a bath in the icy water. He didn't take the dare; instead he said, 'Mother didn't say, "Don't forget to wash" when she made that great long list of Don'ts, did she? So let's wait until somebody tells us to go and wash.' So that was what we did.

We stayed in Wales for weeks and weeks and weeks. Not once in all that time did Mr or Mrs Farmer Jones tell us to go and wash. So we didn't.

We didn't wash our hands or our faces or our knees or our feet or our hair or anything.

At last we had a letter from home. It said:

Dear Rosemary and Francis,
    You will be glad to hear that Daddy is better.
I shall come on Saturday to bring you both
home. I am looking forward to seeing you. I
hope you have been good. Lots of love, until
Saturday,
                    Mummy

We read the letter several times. Mrs Farmer
Jones read it too, and said, 'I think that I had
better give you both a bath on Friday night.'
Mrs Farmer Jones showed us the tin bath tub
which hung on a hook outside the kitchen door.
    On Friday afternoon we were playing a game
throwing pebbles into a puddle in the lane lead-
ing up to the farm. Suddenly our mother came
round the corner. She was a whole day early.
We forgot all about our dirty hair and hands and
faces and ran down the lane to meet her.
    Our mother didn't recognize us at first. Later
she told us that she looked behind her to see if
a filthy, dirty, ragged woman was following her
up the lane, because we were shouting,
'Mummy, Mummy, Mummy' as we ran. It
wasn't until we came up close that she recog-
nized us under all our dirt. She certainly didn't
recognize our clothes, which were ragged and
dirty from the busy time we had had on the

farm.

We didn't go up to the farm. Our mother was cross because we were so dirty. She marched us down to the village, where she bought a towel and a bar of soap. Then she marched us down to the beach. We stood in the sea stark naked. Our mother stood in the sea with her skirt tucked up and scrubbed us from top to bottom with the bar of soap in the cold salty sea. We tingled all over.

When Francis and I were both rubbed dry with the towel our mother began to look more like her smiley old self. We went back to the farm and packed our dirty clothes. We said 'Good-bye' to Mr and Mrs Farmer Jones and set out on the long train journey home.

In the train our mother said, 'I think you were the dirtiest children in the world. I came just in time.'

'But it was wonderful,' said Francis. 'I think I'll be a farmer when I grow up.'

'That's a good idea,' replied our mother, 'as long as you remember to wash sometimes.'

Guess

Philippa Pearce

That last day of October a freak storm hit the suburb of Woodley Park. Slates rattled off roofs, dustbins chased dustbin lids along the streets, hoardings were slammed down, and at midnight there was a huge sound like a giant breaking his kindling wood, and then an almighty crash, and then briefly the sound of the same giant crunching his toast.

Then only the wind, which died surprisingly soon.

In the morning everyone could see that the last forest tree of Grove Road – of the whole suburb – had fallen, crashing down on to Grove Road Primary School. No lives had been lost, since the caretaker did not live on the premises; but the school hamster had later to be treated for shock. The school buildings were wrecked.

Everyone went to stare, especially, of course, the children of the school. They included Netty and Sid Barr.

The fallen tree was an awesome sight, partly because of its size and partly because of its evident great age. Someone in the crowd said that the acorn that grew into *that* must have been planted centuries ago.

As well as the confusion of fallen timber on the road and on the school premises, there was an extraordinary spatter of school everywhere: slates off the roof, bricks from the broken walls, glass from the windows, and the contents of classrooms, cloakrooms and storerooms – books and collages and clay and paints and nature tables and a queer mixture of clothing, both dingy and weird, which meant that the contents of the Lost Property cupboard and the dressing-up cupboard had been whirled together and tossed outside. Any passer-by could have taken his pick, free of charge. Netty Barr, who had been meaning to claim her gym-shoes from Lost Property, decided that they had gone for good now. This was like the end of the world – a school world.

Council workmen arrived with gear to cut, saw and haul timber. Fat old Mr Brown from the end of the Barrs' road told the foreman that they ought to have taken the tree down long ago. Perhaps he was right. In spite of last season's leaves and next year's buds, the trunk of the tree was quite hollow: a cross-section revealed a rim of wood the width of a man's hand, encircling a space large enough for a child or a smallish adult. As soon as the workmen's backs were turned, Sid Barr crept in. He then managed to get stuck and had to be pulled out by Netty. An untidy young woman nearby was convulsed with silent laughter at the incident.

'You didn't stay inside for a hundred years,' she said to Sid.

'That smelt funny,' said Sid. 'Rotty.' Netty banged his clothes for him: the smell clung.

'Remember that day last summer, Net? After the picnic? When I got stuck inside that great old tree in Epping Forest?' Sid liked to recall near-disasters.

'Epping Forest?' said the young woman, sharply interested. But no one else was.

Meanwhile, the headmaster had arrived, and that meant all fun was over. School would go on, after all, even if not in these school buildings for the time being. The pupils of Grove Road were marshalled and then sent off in groups to various other schools in the neighbourhood.

Netty and Sid Barr, with others, went to Stokeside School: Netty in the top class, Sid in a lower one.

There was a good deal of upheaval in Netty's new classroom before everyone had somewhere to sit. Netty was the next-to-last to find a place; the last was a thin, pale girl who chose to sit next to Netty. Netty assumed that she was a Stokesider; yet there was something familiar about her, too. Perhaps she'd just seen her about. The girl had dark, lank hair gathered into a pony tail of sorts, and a pale pointed face with greyish-green eyes. She wore a dingy green dress that looked ready for a jumble sale, and gym-shoes.

Netty studied her sideways. At last, 'You been at Stokeside long?' Netty asked.

The other girl shook her head and glanced at the teacher, who was talking. She didn't seem to want to talk; but Netty did.

'A tree fell on our school,' whispered Netty. The other girl laughed silently, although Netty could see nothing to laugh about. She did see something, however: this girl bore a striking resemblance to the young woman who had watched Sid being pulled from the hollow tree-trunk. The silent laughter clinched the resemblance.

Of course, this girl was much, much younger. Of course.

'How old are you?' whispered Netty.

The girl said a monosyllable, still looking amused.

'What did you say?'

Clearly now: 'Guess.'

Netty was furious: 'I'm just eleven,' she said coldly.

'So am I,' said the other girl.

Netty felt tempted to say 'Liar'; but instead she asked, 'Have you an elder sister?'

'No.'

'What's your name?'

Again that irritating monosyllable. Netty refused to acknowledge it. 'Did you say Jess?' she asked.

'Yes. Jess.'

In spite of what she felt, Netty decided not to argue about that Jess, but went on: 'Jess what?'

The girl looked blank.

'I'm Netty Barr: you're Jess Something – Jess what?'

This time they were getting somewhere: after a tiny hesitation, the girl said, 'Oakes'.

'Jess Oakes. Jessy Oakes.' But whichever way you said it, Netty decided, it didn't sound quite right; and that was because Jess Oakes herself didn't seem quite right. Netty wished now that she weren't sitting next to her.

At playtime Netty went out into the playground; Jess Oakes followed her closely. Netty

didn't like that. Unmistakably, Jess Oakes wanted to stick with her. Why? She hadn't wanted to answer Netty's questions; she hadn't been really friendly. But she clung to Netty. Netty didn't like it – didn't like *her*.

Netty managed to shake Jess Oakes off, but then saw her talking with Sid on the other side of the playground. That made her uneasy. But Jess Oakes did not reappear in the classroom after playtime: Netty felt relieved, although she wondered. The teacher made no remark.

Netty went cheerfully home to tea, a little after Sid.

And there was Jess Oakes sitting with Sid in front of the television set. Netty went into the kitchen, to her mother.

'Here you are,' said Mrs Barr. 'You can take all the teas in.' She was loading a tray.

'When did *she* come?' asked Netty.

'With Sid. Sid said she was your friend.' Netty said nothing. 'She's a lot older than you are, Netty.'

'She's exactly my age. So she says.'

'Well, I suppose with that face and that figure – or that no-figure – she could be any age. Any age.'

'Yes.'

Mrs Barr looked thoughtfully at Netty, put down the breadknife she still held, and with decision set her hands on her hips: 'Netty!'

'Yes?'

'I don't care what age she is, I like your friends better washed than that.'

Netty gaped at her mother.

'She smells,' said Mrs Barr. 'I don't say it's unwashed body, I don't say it's unwashed clothes – although I don't think much of hers. All I know is she smells nasty.'

'Rotty,' said Netty under her breath.

'Don't bring her again,' said Mrs Barr crisply.

Netty took the tea-tray in to the other two. In the semi-dark they all munched and sipped while they watched the TV serial. But Netty was watching Jess Oakes: the girl only seemed to munch and sip; she ate nothing, drank nothing.

A friend called for Sid, and he went out. Mrs Barr looked in to ask if the girls wanted more tea; Netty said no. When her mother had gone, Netty turned off the television and switched on the light. She faced Jess Oakes: 'What do you want?'

The girl's green glance slid away from Netty. 'No harm. To know something.'

'What?'

'The way home.'

Netty did not ask where she had been living, or why she was lost, or any other commonsense questions. They weren't the right questions, she knew. She just said savagely: 'I wish I knew what was going on inside your head, Jess Oakes.'

Jess Oakes laughed almost aloud, as though Netty had said something really amusing. She reached out her hand and touched Netty, for the first time: her touch was cool, damp. 'You shall,' she said. 'You shall.'

And where was Netty now? If she were asleep and dreaming, the falling asleep had been very sudden, at the merest touch of a cool, damp hand. But certainly Netty must be dreaming . . .

She dreamt that she was in a strange room filled with a greenish light that seemed partly to come in through two windows, of curious shape, set together rather low down at one side. The walls and ceilings of this chamber were continuous, as in a dome; all curved. There was nothing inside the dome-shaped chamber except the greenish light, of a curious intensity; and Netty. For some reason Netty wanted to look out of the two windows, but she knew that before she could do that, something was required of her. In her dreaming state, she was not at first sure what this was, except that it was tall – very tall – and green. Of course, green: green in spring and summer, and softly singing to itself with leaves; in autumn, yellow and brown and red, and its leaves falling. In winter, leafless. A tree, a forest tree, a tree of the Forest, a tree of Epping Forest. A tree – a hundred trees – a thousand trees – a choice of all the trees of Epping Forest. She had been to the Forest; she was older than Sid, and therefore she knew the direction in which the Forest lay, the direction in which one would have to go to reach the Forest. Her knowledge of the Forest and its whereabouts was in the green-glowing room, and it passed from her in that room, and became someone else's knowledge too . . .

Now Netty knew that she was free to look out of the windows of the room. Their frames were curiously curved; there was not glass in them, but some other greenish-grey substance. She approached the windows; she looked through them; and she saw into the Barrs' sitting-room, and she saw Netty Barr sitting in her chair by the television set, huddled in sudden sleep.

She saw herself apart from herself, and she cried out in terror, so that she woke, and she was sitting in her chair, and the girl who called herself Jess Oakes was staring at her with her grey-green eyes, smiling.

'Thank you,' said Jess Oakes. 'Now I know all I need to know.' She got up, unmistakably to go. 'Goodbye.'

She went out of the sitting-room, leaving the door open; Netty heard her go out of the front door, leaving that open too. The doors began to bang in a wind that had risen. The front gate banged as well.

Mrs Barr came crossly out of the kitchen to

complain. She saw that Netty was alone in the sitting-room. 'Has she gone, then?'

Netty nodded, dumb.

They went into the hall together. Scattered along the hall were pieces of clothing: one gym-shoe by the sitting-room door, another by the coat-hooks; a dingy green dress, looking like something out of a dressing-up box, by the open front door . . .

Mrs Barr ran to the front gate and looked up and down the road. No one; just old Mr Brown on the lookout, as usual. Mrs Barr called to him: 'Have you seen anyone?'

'No. Who should I have seen?'

Mrs Barr came back, shaken. 'She can't have gone stark naked,' she said. Then, as an after-thought, 'She can't have gone, anyway.' Then again, 'But she has gone.'

Netty was looking at the gym-shoes in the hall. She could see inside one of them; and she could see a name printed there. It would not be JESS OAKES; it would be some other name. Now she would find out the true identity of the girl with the greenish eyes. She stooped, picked up the shoe, read the name: NETTY BARR.

'Those are the gym-shoes you lost at school,' said Mrs Barr. 'How did she get hold of them? Why was she wearing them? What kind of a girl or a woman was she, with that smell on her? Where did she come from? And where's she

gone? Netty, you bad girl, what kind of a friend was she?'

'She wasn't my friend,' said Netty.

'What was she then? And where's she gone – *where's she gone?*'

'I don't know,' said Netty. 'But guess.'

The Terrible Wild Grey Hairy Thing

Jean Chapman

Once a jolly fat Goodie busily made sausages. There was a great pile of them. All kinds of sausages. Long fat ones and long thin ones, short plump tubby sausages and tiny little skinny ones and some that were family-sized which meant that they were bigger than big. King-sized, in fact.

Some of the sausages were spiced with curry, or breathy with garlic, hot with peppers, even red with tomatoes. Others were just plain and meaty, full of pork and beef. All were ready to be sliced and eaten, but not yet . . . these sausages were to last through winter so the Jolly Fat Goodie planned to hang every one from the rafters, high above the kitchen table and well out of reach of the cat.

So each sausage end had a loop of string so it could be hooked over the long nails that were hammered into the rafter beams. Jolly Fat Goodie would not wait for her husband to come in from the fields and hang the sausages. No. She must do the job herself and because she was not much taller than she was wide, up she climbed on the kitchen table, and by stretching and wobbling on tiptoes she managed to hook a sausage to a nail. And so she worked steadily until there were bunches of hooked sausages dangling above her head.

By then Goodie was red-faced and hot, but pleased with herself. Then, just as she wobbled and stretched to hang the biggest of the family-sized sausages, the king of them all – calamity! Jolly Fat Baby, who plodded about on the floor, trod on the cat. *Ourrr*! The cat screamed and escaped from the baby in a long scuttling run and a wild leap. It landed on the table where it brushed by teetering Goodie's leg. Hardly more than a whisker tickled Goodie but it was enough to bounce her off the table. Down she thudded, taking the remaining sausages with her.

Sausages seemed to fly about the room. They went everywhere. Any wonder the Jolly Fat Baby bawled with fright, and just as well Goodie was unhurt, if a little puffed. She scooped up her child and gave him one hundred kisses. And the poor cat? Long gone – out of the door so the Jolly Fat Goodie had no idea what had caused that split-second disaster.

Before long she picked up the sausages. There were plenty of them scattered over the floor. And one stuck out of the bread crock . . . two poised on the saucepan shelf . . . three lolled on a chair and none were on the table. She didn't notice the stray, the biggest family-sized, the king of sausages that lay wedged behind a heavy tool chest. She didn't miss it because Jolly Fat Goodie had not fussed and counted her sausages.

There it stayed, gathering dust and floor sweepings. Goodie was not too fussy about housekeeping either and didn't sweep behind the chest all winter. Once, when the chest was opened her Jolly Fat Husband shoved it a little closer to the wall. The sausage silently squashed. The skin slit a little and the sausage changed its shape to a little less round, a little longer, a little flatter and a little thinner with a few bumps.

Several times the cat investigated the delicious smell behind the tool chest but she couldn't squeeze herself into the space. She was a jolly fat cat and her legs were too short and her claws too blunt to haul out the sausage. She had to give up her dream of a sausage snack.

'There's a funny pong in this house!' complained the Jolly Fat Husband some weeks later. He had just come in from the bracing fresh air of the fields. 'Yes, something is a bit off,' agreed Goodie, wriggling her nose with distaste.

They used their noses then to hunt the smell; sniffing the baby, sniffing the cat, sniffing the stove and cupboard, sniffing in corners and never sniffing out the stray sausage. Of course, it was the reason for the smell but there it stayed behind the tool chest.

Just as well winter was at its end. Goodie opened wide the door and windows to let in the sun and scents of spring. The strange smell either wafted out on the draughts, or they had become used to it. Certainly it no longer worried them.

The sausage stayed where it was: a long flattish lumpy object now and difficult to see had you happened to peer into the gloom behind the chest. As well, grey mould with long hairy whiskers had sprouted from the sausage skin and the whiskers, that were finer than the cat's, were powdered with dust.

By now Jolly Fat Goodie was busy with her spring-cleaning. She whacked dust from mats, washed blankets, aired mattresses and refilled pillows. Out came her broom, scrubbing brush, mop and bucket. Goodie swept and scrubbed, pulling the bed from the wall and piling chairs on the table out of her way. She couldn't, however, shift the heavy tool box alone and she would have ignored it altogether if her Jolly Fat Husband hadn't happened to return from the fields. He couldn't move it either – goodness knows what was in it. Both of them had to shove and push together, shove and push until it suddenly slid away from the wall.

Goodie shrieked.

Jolly Fat Husband snatched her broom.

'Don't touch it!' shrilled Goodie and she grabbed his arm with both hands so that he couldn't strike the terrible wild grey hairy thing lurking behind the chest. 'It might bite,' she whispered.

Jolly Fat Husband dropped the broom at once. Goodie snatched up her Jolly Fat Baby. They backed to the stove, huddling with thumping hearts to peer at the terrible wild grey hairy thing waiting in the shadows. 'What is it?' breathed Goodie. 'A wild animal?'

'I've never seen anything like it before,' gasped her husband with his eyes riveted on the thing. It hadn't moved. 'Look here! I'll have to get help.'

'Don't leave me,' pleaded Goodie but he told her that he must, and shepherded Goodie and their baby to the bedroom, never once taking his eyes off the skulking thing, just waiting to attack.

Quietly, cautiously, he shut the bedroom door and crept from the kitchen, then he ran, yelling to the neighbours.

Goodie hurriedly latched the bedroom door. All nervous fingers and fumbling thumbs she stuffed the eiderdown along the bottom of the door, then pushed their big bed against it while the baby bounced and gurgled in the middle of the bed, enjoying himself.

Soon Goodie heard men stomping to the house and she crouched on a pillow to squint through the keyhole.

Most of the neighbours had crowded to the kitchen door, all armed with hay forks and shovels, spades and garden rakes, crowbars and axes. Necks craned for a glimpse of the terrible wild grey hairy thing. They gasped and shuddered and declared they had never seen the like.

Then along came Squire with his gun, shouldering his way through the men, stamping and shouting, 'Where is it? Let me see. Make way. I'll shoot it dead.'

His eyes fell on the terrible wild grey hairy thing and he was sure that he saw a long tail flick – that was Goodie's sausage string. And he was positive that a mean eye glared at him – that was a speck of white sausage lard gleaming through a thin patch of mould, and Squire stared at it, mesmerized, unable to move, but for one moment only.

And during that silent and seemingly long moment a daring young lad reached out, and before anyone could stop him, his stick prodded at the terrible wild grey hairy thing. It rolled over. Squire and the rest of them fell away from the door, backing and tripping, scurrying and shoving in a fast retreat. Every man was certain that it had growled and was after him, spitting poison and hatred!

Squire recovered first. He had been in the army once. He ordered the men to stay calm. He had a plan. Everyone must help. 'We'll frighten the enemy from the house,' he bellowed. 'We'll make a great row. That'll get him moving,' he roared. Squire must have been a sergeant in the army as all the village heard the instructions.

An uproar followed. People shouted and yelled, clanged pots, hit sticks and belted the side of the house until Jolly Fat Goodie heard her cups and plates rattling on the shelves. 'Stop! Stop!' she screeched in fury from the window but no one heard her above the din, or the baby either. He roared because he didn't like the noise. Neither did the cat. She ran off. Neither did the hens. They squawked but dogs came from everywhere, yapping and barking. And through it all the terrible wild grey hairy thing lurked by the chest as if it were stone-deaf. Not a move did it make, not an eye blink or a tail twitch.

'Louder!' encouraged Squire. 'Louder!'

At that very shout a black dog ran silently between men's legs and then through Squire's. Squire toppled sideways to knock against Jolly Fat Husband. They clutched each other in a bear hug dancing in hops, trying to balance but it was of little use. Down they crashed in an undignified heap while the dog ran on, up over the step, through the door, into the kitchen. It attacked the terrible wild grey hairy thing with its teeth.

There was a breathless shocked silence. Eyes rounded or bulged as the dog gulped, gobbled, slurped and chewed, then swallowed. He killed the thing and ate it! *Ate it*! Even Squire couldn't believe that it was gone, gone in a flash. That dog was a hero!

Now there was a fresh uproar. Who owned this brave dog? No one? Surely it wasn't a stray? Indeed it was, and everyone wanted to keep it. Squire very nearly did because he was important and had been in the army, possibly as a sergeant. And he may have won the black dog but Goodie rewarded it with the fattest garlic sausage hanging from the rafters. Of course, the dog refused to leave her, so Squire gave it a medal which it casually wore on its fine leather collar, also a present from Squire.

Only the brave dog knew that he had eaten a family-sized sausage, the king of them all. However, the terrible wild grey hairy thing was long talked about as an invading monster.

The Turbulent Term of Tyke Tiler

Gene Kemp

This is the way it all began with me and Danny. I had to get him to follow me. He'd never forgive himself otherwise.

'But I tell you it's a real skellinton, Tyke. I tell you where I seen it. Down in the leat. I went there yesterday when you was out. Come on. Come and look. I bet it's somebody what's bin murdered.'

'I got into enough trouble over that marrow bone . . .'

81

But Danny had set off along the road as if he was warming up for the fifteen hundred metres. He belted down the bank, where the old city walls stand, that drops down to the river and the leats, the oldest part of the city, Sir says. I soon caught up with him, Crumble at my heels, her ears ruffling out in the wind.

'Which leat are the bones in?'

There are two, Cricklepit and Walter, that cut off from the river below the weir. The leats and the river make an island that's mostly a deserted place. Danny panted:

'By the bridge. Near the warehouses.'

'They weren't there last week.'

'The rain and high water brung 'em out.'

We ran on, past the old, broken water-wheel, hidden in the trees and bushes, where the king-fisher flies sometimes. I've seen him quite a lot lately. I threw a broken brick into the water sluicing through an iron grid. The brown colour had gone but it was still high. Everywhere was quiet. No one comes round here much. Every-thing's either being knocked down or rotting away; it's a place for secrets and adventures.

Perhaps this was an adventure. Perhaps the bones were the skeleton of a murdered man, or valuable prehistoric remains. We ran through the square where my Gran used to live before it was demolished and on to a little sandstone bridge. Beside it was a wall and a railing and a long drop to the leat. We climbed over and inspected the filthy water.

'There. There it is.'

Danny pointed at what looked like a huge set of teeth decorated with floating strands of green slime. Other bones were scattered around. Crumble made eeking noises on the other side of the wall, so I lifted her over.

'It's lovely, Tyke.'

'It's a sheep, you nutter. It's like that one Martin Kneeshaw brought off the moor and went round showing off.'

'No it's not. It's a man, I tell you. Somebody murdered that man and chucked his body in here and he mouldered and mouldered away till he was that skellinton.'

'It's a sheep . . .'

He took no notice.

'We'll be on telly. Danny Price and Tyke Tiler found a murdered skellinton. Do you think there'll be a reward?' Crumble ran up and down the muddy bank, taking great interest in the bones as well. I didn't think she would leap off the bank, though, as it was a long way down to the water.

'You must know it's a sheep, Danny . . .' but he wasn't listening. His face was white and his eyes glittered. Completely nutty . . . mad as a snake . . . absolutely bonkers.

'Get it for me, Tyke.'

'What?'

'Get it for me. I want it.'

'You gotter be joking.'

'You get it for me, Tyke.'

'Get stuffed.'

'Please.'

I looked at the dirty, scummy water. This leat always got choked up, yet in the centre the current ran fast and fierce. Danny gazed at the bones as if they were the Crown Jewels.

'My Mum will wallop me if I get mucky again. She said so.'

'I want them bones.'

'Get 'em, then.'

'It's too steep for me.'

'Then it's too steep for me, too!'

'But you're clever. You can do anything.'

'Gee t'anks. For nothing.'

'If I take it to school I'll get some house points.'

'I thought you wanted to be famous. You won't get on the telly with sheep's teeth and house points. Make up your mind.'

'If it's a murdered man's skellinton, then I'll go on the telly and be famous, and if it's a sheep's I'll get some house points.'

He was starting to talk faster and faster and suddenly I thought maybe he'd gone completely bonkers, and I'd better humour him, so I said what about some chips because I'm starving and

I could fix him up with some fossils to take to school instead.

He wasn't listening.

'Get them bones for me, Tyke.'

'I don't want to . . .' and then I stopped. You can't get through to Danny when he's got an idea in his head, for there's only room for one at a time. I studied the water down below. The bottom was covered with broken bricks over which lay tins, bits of metal, sticks and wire, and the bones veiled in their green slime drifting and weaving in the current. It looked pretty deep. I wasn't likely to get drowned here – not like the river – but it looked cold and unfriendly. I thought of me Mum, and I looked at Danny still gazing at the bones and talking. Holding on to a tree root I lowered myself into the mucky, muddy, slimy water. It didn't seem worth taking my shoes and socks off as my trousers would get soaked anyway. Anyway I'd got my doom feeling by now. My doom feeling is when I know I'm slap bang in the middle of something that will lead to trouble, but I can't stop doing it all the same. I could hear my Gran saying:

'You might as well be hung for a sheep as a lamb.'

She used to say a lot of things like that.

Danny danced about on the edge of the bank.

'That's it, Tyke. You've nearly got 'em.'

There was a slithering noise, and an enormous

splash. A piece of weed hit me on the nose and I was wet all over. Crumble had arrived to help. She lifted her nose in the air and started to swim, back legs kicking hard. She flurried all the water and I lost the bones. I couldn't see a thing.

'You stupid fool of a dog, get out,' I yelled. She swam round and round me, nose in the air. The water was icy even through shoes, socks and trousers. I reached into the mud and found the bones.

'It's the teethy ones I want,' Danny jumped up and down.

'It stinks!'

It was slimily, horribly soft to the touch as well, a yellow jawbone with long teeth. I moved to the bank to hand it up to Danny. Crumble tried to follow this delightful pong and, getting to the bank, snapped at the teeth, then fell back into the water again.

'And the rest,' Danny roared, hopping, by now.

I got the rest. They felt really horrible. They smelt worse.

Danny cradled them in his arms, making little humming noises.

'I got a bag,' he said, bringing one out of his pocket. He put the bones in it and gathered it to his chest. The bag went soggy. Crumble and I started to climb the bank. Danny went over the wall.

'Hey! Gimme a hand!'

He managed to remember me for a moment and stretched out a mitt, but the bank was so churned up with all his leaping about that he suddenly slipped, and fell flat on his back, bones clasped to his chest.

Down I crashed on to the slimy stones in that stinking leat. Crumble joined me, licking my face as I tried to get to my feet. Danny Price sat on the bank, laughing like a drain.

Wild with fury, I travelled up that bank at a thousand miles per hour, dragging Crumble by her collar.

'I'm gonna exterminate you, and bury you with your rotten ole bones!'

I've got twice his speed, but sopping wet trousers and squelching shoes don't help. Crumble kept running in and out of my legs. I gave up and headed for home instead.

Linda Stoatway watched from her doorway.

'You a mermaid, eh, Tyke?' she giggled and collapsed on Lorraine Fairchild standing beside her.

I tried to get in without being seen, through the back door and up to the bathroom, as quiet as a mouse with rubber boots on. Crumble I left outside to dry off, I hoped.

Only at that moment me Mum had just taken Aunt Marge to view our new posh lilac bath. Aunt Marge needn't have screamed as loud as she did. I've never liked her. Afterwards Mum said it was that scream just as much as the sight of me soaked in slime that upset her.

Danny got his house points, but after a day Sir said he couldn't bear the smell any longer and would we take the bones away. We did.

We took them to the leat and threw them in. I stopped Crumble from jumping in after them.

'I think them teeth are grinning at us,' said Danny.

'I wouldn't be at all surprised,' I replied.

Dad says he hates the new lilac bath and Mum must've been mad to choose such a colour.

Acknowledgements

The editors and publishers would like to thank the following for permission to use copyright material in this collection. The publishers have made every effort to contact the copyright holders but there are a few cases where it has not been possible to do so. We would be grateful to hear from anyone who can enable us to contact them so the omission can be corrected at the first opportunity.

Ashton Scholastic for 'The Terrible Wild Grey Hairy Thing' by Jean Chapman. Copyright © Jean Chapman. Jonathan Cape Ltd and Penguin Books Ltd for 'How to Recognize a Witch' by Roald Dahl from *The Witches*. Copyright © Roald Dahl.
J. M. Dent & Sons Ltd for 'The Chewing-Gum Rescue' by Margaret Mahy from *The Chewing-Gum Rescue and Other Stories*. Copyright © Margaret Mahy.
Andre Deutsch Ltd for 'The Story of Giant Kippernose' by John Cunliffe from *Giant Kippernose and Other Stories*. Copyright © John Cunliffe.
Faber & Faber Ltd for 'Toothie and Cat' by Gene Kemp from *Dog Days and Cat Naps*; and the extract from *The Turbulent Term of Tyke Tiler* by Gene Kemp. Copyright © Gene Kemp.
Farrar, Straus & Giroux, Inc for 'Rattlesnake Soup' by Philip Ashton Rollins from *Gone Haywire*. Copyright © Charles Scribner's Sons.
Hutchinson Children's Books Ltd for 'Did I Ever Tell You . . . About the Dirtiest Children in the World' by